J

KEISHA LEADS THE WAY
by Teresa Reed

Illustrations by
Eric Velasquez

Spot Illustrations by
Rich Grote

MagicAttic Club

MAGIC ATTIC PRESS

Published by Magic Attic Press.

For more information contact:
Book Editor, Magic Attic Press, 866 Spring Street,
P.O. Box 9722, Portland, ME 04104-5022.

First Edition
Printed in the United States of America
2 3 4 5 6 7 8 9 10

Betsy Gould, Publisher
Marva Martin, Art Director
Robin Haywood, Managing Editor

Edited by Judit Bodnar
Designed by Susi Oberhelman

ISBN 1-57513-017-3

Magic Attic Club books are printed on acid-free, recycled paper.

As members of the
MAGIC ATTIC CLUB,
we promise to
be best friends,
share all of our adventures in the attic,
use our imaginations,
have lots of fun together,
and remember—the real magic is in us.

Alison   *Keisha*

Heather   *Megan*

Contents

EMERGENCY CALL!

This is going to be the best week ever," sighed Keisha Vance, falling back against the purple pillows on her bed. A few cookies slid from the tray beside her, and she lazily handed them to her friends. The Sunday afternoon sun lit the room softly through her lavender-and-white-checked curtains.

"I'll say," said Megan Ryder. "I've been looking forward to our social studies test all year."

There was complete silence for a moment as everyone

stared at Megan. Then the girls burst into laughter. "Oh, Megan!" Keisha exclaimed. "You get me every time with that straight face. I always fall for it."

When Heather Hardin stopped laughing, she asked, "How can you say something like that without cracking up?"

"Actually, I *am* looking forward to the test," said Megan, glancing at Alison, "and I've been studying, too."

Alison McCann gave a little pout. "I know, I know. I'm going to start studying this afternoon, I promise. But Megan, you know Keisha wasn't talking about schoolwork."

Keisha grinned. "I'm talking about the volunteer day that Ms. Austin set up. I think it's her best idea yet. We're finally going to get a chance to do something important."

"And we've all got incredible things to do," said Heather as she started doing ballet exercises in the middle of Keisha's bedroom. "I'm so excited about working at the day care center, I don't know how I'm going to wait until Wednesday."

"Me either," said Alison. "I can't believe Ms. Austin actually gave me my dream assignment. I mean, there I was, holding my breath and hoping I would get the animal shelter, and I did!"

"I know you guys don't think my 'job' is so great," said Megan, "but the recycling center really matters. People need to think seriously about the environment."

"Megan, nobody here thinks that's a boring assignment at all," said Keisha. "The recycling center is terrific. Remember how long it took to get it?"

"I sure do," Megan answered, obviously pleased that her friend agreed. "Say, Keisha, aren't you glad you get to volunteer at the hospital?"

Keisha sat up a little straighter on her bed and then stretched forward, touching her chin to her knees. "At first I wasn't so sure it was a good idea. I mean, sometimes it seems like everything that happens in this family has to do with the hospital."

Heather kneeled at the foot of Keisha's bed. "You mean because your mom's a nurse in the maternity ward?"

"Right. And with Dad being an administrator, they both spend so much time there. So I decided it would be good for me to see what really goes on."

"Your parents do work a lot," Alison said sympathetically as she grabbed an oatmeal cookie from the tray. She picked a few crumbs off the lavender polka-dot quilt and dropped them on the tray, then sat down beside Keisha.

Keisha gave a little sigh. "Don't get me wrong. My parents have really important jobs and I'm proud of them. But sometimes it seems as though I don't do

anything but baby-sit my little sister and brother, and anybody can do that."

Megan folded her legs Indian-style and looked at Keisha. "What do you think you'll get to do at the hospital?"

"I figure since they know my mom and dad, they'll put me where they really need help, like the children's ward."

"You really think you'll get to work there?" Heather asked.

"Why not? Mom said she spoke to Mrs. Livingston, who's in charge of our class volunteers for the day. I just know she'll give me something special."

Alison tapped her friend on the ankle. "You've got *two* good things happening to you this week. Your dad's coming to visit our class."

"I know, and I think he's even more excited than I am. You should have seen his face when Ms. Austin asked if he would talk to our class about being a volunteer paramedic."

Suddenly Mr. Vance's pager started beeping downstairs, and Keisha heard her father bounding up the stairs.

Keisha jumped up and peeked out the door. She wanted to hear the conversation, but her father walked into her parents' bedroom and shut the door.

"What's up, Keish?" Heather asked. "Is your father on call with the emergency medical unit this weekend?"

"Yes, he is." Keisha frowned. "Whenever that beeper goes off, he has to drop everything and get to the scene as fast as possible."

"Wow! It's really loud," said Alison.

"Well, that's the point," Megan said. "If you're a volunteer, you have to be reachable no matter where you are."

"Why don't people just go straight to the hospital?" Heather asked.

"They might need medical care before they can be moved," Keisha explained, "like if they had a heart attack or broke a leg. Or sometimes people are home alone and need help to get to the hospital."

"Keisha, it's so cool that both your parents do work that actually saves people's lives," said Heather.

"That's why I want to show them that I can do something really important and help people, too."

Keisha's friends nodded in agreement. "It's going to be a great day for all of us," said Alison.

"Volunteer day, here we come!" the girls shouted all together.

Chapter Two

DAD'S VISIT

That Tuesday, Keisha looked on proudly as her father told the class about his work as a volunteer paramedic. It was the last period of the day, when students were usually getting restless; but to Keisha's delight, everyone listened intently.

Noah Cummings raised his hand. "What's the most exciting thing that ever happened?"

"I was thinking about that," said Mr. Vance, smiling. "Just recently, we got a call from 911 that a woman was trapped in an elevator in a building near the airport. Everyone was frantic because the woman was alone in the elevator and having labor pains." The whole class let out a gasp.

"What did you do?" Heather blurted out.

"First we tried to get the woman out of the elevator, which was halfway between floors. She was being really calm about everything, but we could hear that she was having a rough time. The thing was, the emergency release for the doors didn't work. No matter what we tried, we couldn't get those doors open."

Mr. Vance paused for a moment, and Keisha glanced around the room. She had hardly ever seen the class pay such close attention to anyone.

"While my partner worked on the sixth-floor doors, I ran upstairs to the seventh floor and unlocked those elevator doors. Thank goodness the emergency key worked! Then I had to jump a few feet down the shaft and land on top of the elevator."

Wows and aahs echoed through the classroom.

"Luckily, the elevator was relatively new, so it was built with stabilizers that older elevators don't always have. They kept the elevator car from swinging back and forth when I landed."

"How did you get inside?" asked Ms. Austin.

"All elevators have a trap door in the roof just for situations like this and to provide access to the cable lines," Mr. Vance replied. "I opened the trap door and swung down into the car. The woman was very worried about getting to the hospital, and I had to spend a few minutes assuring her that everything was going to be okay. In the meantime, my partner and I did everything we could, but we still only managed to get the doors open a few inches.

"Now, the elevator repairman had been called, of course. It's just that they can't rush right over, the way paramedics do. By the time the repairman showed up, the woman was clutching her stomach and saying that the baby was going to come any minute. Well, I could see that she knew what she was talking about. So I had my partner pass the first aid kit and some towels, blankets, and a pillow through the opening. I helped the woman get as comfortable as possible while my partner and the repairman worked on the elevator—but they weren't fast enough.

"By the time the elevator was moving and level with the floor and the doors were opened, the woman had given birth to a healthy baby girl."

"Wow!" Alison gasped out loud. The rest of the class was speechless for a minute, then burst into applause and gathered around Mr. Vance.

Keisha edged through the crowd to the front of the room and tried to get her father's attention. "Daddy, you were great!" she said. But he was surrounded by her classmates asking questions and he didn't seem to hear her.

Keisha turned to Brittany Foster. "Someday I'm going to save people just like my dad does. I might even—"

Brittany interrupted her. "Listen, Keisha, do you think I could come over and talk to your dad about being a paramedic? I'm doing a paper on emergency services, and he might be able to give me some information."

"Oh, sure, just ask him. He'd be happy to help you," said Keisha. With that, Brittany turned away. Then someone punched Keisha's arm lightly.

"What a story!" Alison exclaimed. "I bet you wish you could be a hero like your dad."

"I do all kinds of heroic things already!" Keisha answered, sounding a little snippier than she meant to. "I baby-sit Ashley and Ronnie all the time by myself. When Ashley got that really bad cut, who do you think

took care of it? And . . ." Keisha couldn't think of anything else right then, but there were other important things she'd done— plenty of them.

"But you didn't actually save someone's life," Alison replied with a raised eyebrow.

Keisha didn't feel like arguing. Instead, she concentrated on trying to get her father's attention. When she finally got close enough to say something, though, Ms. Austin came up with her appointment book and started talking to him.

At last Keisha's father tapped her on the shoulder. "Why don't you round up your friends and I'll give everyone a ride home," he suggested.

Keisha was about to say they'd rather walk, when Alison piped up. "Oh, thanks, Mr. Vance. I'll get Megan and Heather and we'll meet you at your car." As Keisha followed her father into the hallway, her classmates were still thanking him. Keisha ran to the car and hopped into the front seat, and her friends climbed into the back.

Megan leaned forward and stuck her head between Keisha and her father. "Mr. Vance, we'd love to hear some more of your rescue stories."

The words stung Keisha. She was relieved when the car finally turned up her street. Usually she was glad that her friends lived so close, but at that moment, what she wanted was to get away.

In the kitchen, Ronnie's and Ashley's shrieks and giggles sounded unusually loud. Keisha gave her mom a quick kiss hello—and barely missed being tackled by Ronnie as he hurled himself at their father.

"Mom, may I go over to Ellie's for awhile?" Keisha asked quietly. When Keisha, Heather, Megan, and Alison had met their silver-haired neighbor during winter vacation, they'd found more than a fascinating older friend. Ellie Goodwin had let the girls explore her attic, which was full of interesting items from her travels. Best of all, there seemed to be an endless variety of exotic clothing. Whenever they tried on an outfit in front of the attic's gilt-edged mirror, they found themselves in an amazing adventure. They had formed the Magic Attic Club right after their first trip. The girls could return to the attic whenever they wanted excitement and surprise—or just to get away from things—and sharing their adventures had brought them even closer together than before.

Keisha's parents were deep in conversation. Obviously, her mother hadn't heard the question.

"Mom!" Keisha yelled.

The entire family fell silent and stared at Keisha.

"Sorry. I just wanted to know if I could go over to Ellie's before dinner."

"That's fine, Keisha. Just make sure you're back here at six-thirty."

Keisha hurried out of the house before her parents could say anything else.

Chapter Three

GOING TO AFRICA

Keisha ran up the steps to Ellie's door and rang the bell. "Keisha!" Ellie cried when she opened the door, wiping one hand on a rag that hung from her pocket.

"Hi, Ellie," said Keisha, eyeing Ellie's smock and the artist's palette in her hand. "Did I interrupt you? I can come back another time if you're busy."

"Oh, not at all, my dear," said Ellie. "Come in, come in. I'd like to get your opinion on my latest masterpiece."

Keisha followed Ellie past the parlor and dining room, across the kitchen, and through a door at the back. She found herself in a large, sun-drenched studio whose wide, open bay windows looked out onto Ellie's orderly garden. A fresh breeze stirred the sheer white curtains. The smells of mint and oil paint filled the air.

"Oh, what a beautiful room!" Keisha exclaimed. Even after all her visits, she hadn't known this part of Ellie's house existed.

"I'm glad you like it. I have to admit, it is one of my favorite rooms. Here, have a look at my painting."

Keisha walked over to the easel in the middle of the room. A small table covered with messy-looking tubes of paint stood next to it. Keisha stared at the canvas, which showed a sketch of a small African village.

"Ellie, have you been to Africa?"

"Oh, yes, several times. This is a painting of my favorite place, a village in the rain forest section of the Zaire River basin. I was just about to take a break. Would you care to join me?"

"That's right," Keisha giggled. "I forgot it was teatime!"

"Make yourself comfortable, my dear." With a smile, Ellie gestured to the cushioned window seat. "Let me just fetch a glass for you."

Keisha took Ellie at
her word, removing her
sneakers and curling up
on the striped velvety
cushion.  Scones and a pitcher of iced tea were already set
out within easy reach on a low table.

"Now, wasn't this your father's day to speak to your
class?" asked Ellie, handing Keisha a glass of peppermint
iced tea. "How did it go?"

"Okay, I guess," answered Keisha. Ellie gave her a
quizzical look, and before Keisha knew it, she was telling
Ellie everything about the afternoon—even the part about
being a little envious that her friends at school were so
impressed by her father's rescue stories. Ellie didn't say
much, but that was one of the things Keisha liked about
her. Most of the time Ellie just listened.

While Keisha finished her second scone, Ellie poured
herself another glass of tea. Keisha walked across the
room to look at the painting again. "I've always wanted to
go to Africa," she said.

"Sometime when you're upstairs, you should have a
look around, my dear. I have a number of African mementos
throughout the house, but I think you might be particularly
interested in some special treasures in the attic."

"Oh, could I go now? I won't be long. And then I'd like to hear all about your travels through Zaire."

"Of course," said Ellie as Keisha grabbed her sneakers.

Keisha skipped back down the hallway and took the attic key from its silver box on the table in the front hall. The key slid smoothly into the lock. She hurried up the attic stairs and turned on the light.

Keisha eagerly wandered around the attic, peeking into drawers and small cubbyholes in Ellie's rolltop desk and opening cardboard cartons. There were fabrics in all sorts of weaves and colors, and a whole boxful of bright, bold African cotton prints. Some of the boxes held books in languages Keisha didn't recognize, and there were several collections of seashells and polished stones.

In a wooden box in one corner, Keisha found half a dozen African statues. The wood was satiny, as if many people's hands had rubbed it again and again. Then she took out several masks. They all looked very old. Keisha delicately stroked the wood, careful not to damage their brittle-looking straw hair. A few of the masks were smooth like the statues, and others were very rough and grainy. A couple were pretty scary-looking. Keisha could hardly wait to ask Ellie about them.

But first Keisha had to check Ellie's enormous steamer trunk. As soon as she lifted the heavy lid, a pattern of bright, strong colors caught her eye. She gently tugged on the fabric until she was able to pull the whole outfit out of the trunk. It was an African robe! Keisha laid it on a small chair beside the trunk and returned to her search. Soon she found a beautiful gold-colored headdress and matching collar, then a pair of golden sandals and a whole handful of bead bracelets.

Keisha stood at the mirror and put on the outfit piece by piece, saving the collar and headdress for last. She fastened the collar around her neck and settled it just so, then untied her ponytail and carefully placed the crown over her hair.

"I must be a princess," she whispered. "A real live princess from Africa." She gazed into the mirror, and as she wondered aloud, "Exactly where will I end up?" her reflection disappeared.

Keisha heard a sharp clucking and found herself surrounded by several large purple and gray birds. She backed off and looked around, a bit dazed. She was standing just outside a high, curving wall made of woven straw. Several small thatched huts were visible through the entrance, which had no door or gate. Lush trees, some of them hundreds of feet tall, and plants she didn't recognize completely surrounded the clearing.

"Shoo! Shoo, you silly *nkanga* birds! Leave poor
Keisha alone," cried a tall, graceful woman. She leaped
after the bird, her bare feet stirring up small clouds of
dust on the ground as she chased it through the opening
in the wall. The woman wore a long dress made of boldly
colored fabric that appeared to be made of strips
wrapped around her body. She gave a last flap of her
arms and turned to Keisha. "And since when is the
mukumu's daughter afraid of guinea fowl?" she demanded.

To Keisha's surprise, she understood what the woman
meant. The chief's daughter? she wondered, looking
around. She means me, she said to herself.

Keisha's train of thought was broken by loud giggling.
She caught a glimpse of several girls her own age ducking
their heads back through the
opening in the wall. Then
she looked again at the
woman, who was now
standing with her
hands on her hips.

"Keisha, you are
staring at me as if you
don't recognize your
own aunt. Where have you

26

been? And why are you wearing your ceremonial crown and collar? Even *you* have duties, you know."

"I—I went for a walk," Keisha stammered.

"You went for a walk in your ceremonial robes?" cried the woman, bending to pick up a large, sand-colored bowl from beside the wall. "You were supposed to be looking after your little cousin Sofi. Have you forgotten that you are her nurse-sibling? I had to get one of the other girls to watch her."

Keisha was supposed to be baby-sitting! Well, that was something she was familiar with, anyhow. Even though it wasn't her fault—she couldn't exactly explain that she just got there—Keisha felt bad and hung her head. "I'm sorry," she murmured.

"How can you go walking when there is so much to prepare for the men's departure? Well, hurry inside," the woman replied.

Keisha followed her through the gate.

Chapter Four

THE MUKUMU'S DAUGHTER

It's a real village!" Keisha exclaimed in wonder as she stepped inside. She caught herself immediately and looked up to see if the woman had heard. But the woman—her aunt, it seemed—continued walking, stopping only to adjust the bowl that she balanced on her head. Keisha relaxed a little and looked around.

The wall was about the shape and size of the one around the football field behind the high school. There were small thatch-roofed huts along the wall, separated every few feet by vegetable and flower gardens. In the middle of the compound, four larger huts shared the shade of a large plantain tree where a few ancient-looking men squatted.

Keisha and the woman made their way among the goats and chickens and *nkanga* that milled about the dusty yard. At the back of the compound, several old women were sitting on the ground, rocking infants in their laps and fanning them with flyswatters while toddlers tumbled around them.

Keisha's "aunt" stopped and set her bowl down next to a small group of women about her age. Then she knelt beside a long, deep trough filled with water, took a handful of thick reeds from a nearby stack, and set them in the water. She and the women began talking very fast. Until then, Keisha had been so caught up in surveying her new surroundings that she hadn't had time to think about the strange language or wonder how she understood it.

She stood and watched the women making a cane chair. Their fingers flew in and out and around the frame, filling in the outline with several shades of yellow and brown leaves and reeds. Keisha's aunt stirred the water, making sure the reeds soaked evenly.

One of the women looked over at her and smiled. "The throne will be ready for the harvest festival, Keisha," she said, "so you can sit beside your father when he gives thanks."

"*Ewe*, Keisha! Over here!" A pretty girl waved to Keisha. She was tall and thin, about the same age as Keisha, with dark skin and hair and slanted golden-brown eyes. Around her, Keisha saw some of the girls who had run off earlier when the woman scolded her. Now they sat chatting and giggling while they wove baskets of various shapes and sizes.

Keisha waved back gratefully and hurried over, taking off her crown and collar and jewelry. As she bent down to join the circle, a little girl about her sister Ashley's age rushed over and threw her tiny arms around Keisha's neck. She caught Keisha off balance, and everyone laughed when the two of them fell down.

"Kee-Kee, you left me!" cried the little girl, hugging even tighter. Keisha couldn't believe her ears. "Kee-Kee" was what her brother, Ronnie, always called her!

"I'm sorry, Sofi. I didn't leave you on purpose," said Keisha, hoping this was the girl her aunt had mentioned.

"Well, Wiri played with me all day, but you were bad to leave me alone. You are my nurse-sibling, not Wiri."

"*Jambo*, Keisha. What happened to you today?" Wiri asked. "You know I didn't mind watching Sofi for you. I just wish you'd told me where you were going. Mama Loma questioned me all day long." She looked pointedly at the woman who had brought Keisha inside the village compound.

This girl must be Wiri, thought Keisha, and Mama Loma must be my "aunt."

"I'm sorry," Keisha said. "I guess I just decided at the last minute to leave. Thanks for taking care of Sofi."

Wiri shook her head and laughed. "Keisha, we never know what you are going to do from day to day. I suppose that's the luck of being the *mukumu*'s daughter."

A mixture of thrill and fear shot through Keisha. If she was the chief's daughter, what was expected of her?

Suddenly Keisha realized that Mama Loma was by her side and that some of the women had joined the girls, helping them to weave. The steady, rhythmic motions that Mama Loma showed her were calming. Before she knew it, Keisha had learned everyone's name, and she was able to join in the talk and to laugh with the others.

The old women stayed by themselves with the babies and toddlers. Keisha watched in fascination as a group of boys and girls ran past the weavers and through the group of elderly women. They called all the women *mama*—"mother"—or *bibi*—"grandmother"—and Keisha couldn't tell which children belonged to which women.

Mama Loma stood up and began brushing off her dress. In a flash, one of the women handed a basket to a girl who couldn't have been more than eight years old. Keisha watched in awe as the girl walked away with it balanced perfectly on her head.

Wiri leaned close to Keisha and asked, "Has Mbele mentioned which way he and your brothers will take the men tomorrow? This is the first time our people have looked for new land since you and I were babies."

Keisha had no idea who Mbele was or what Wiri was talking about, so she shrugged and shook her head.

Little Sofi frowned. "I don't want to move to a strange new place," she said softly. The other young children clustered around their nurse-siblings, their eyes wide and their lips pursed in frowns.

"Don't worry, children," said Mama Loma. "You know we move whenever the land is exhausted and we cannot grow good crops anymore. With his sons and the other men, Mukumu Mbele will find a good place for our new home." Her calm voice and matter-of-fact manner seemed to reassure the little ones.

"All right," Mama Loma continued. "It's time to get supper ready. The men will be back from the fields soon, and our weaving and caning are done for today." The women gathered the reeds and canes and took them away.

I guess "Mbele" is the name of my father, Keisha thought, and he's going to lead the search tomorrow. She turned to Wiri and asked, "What time do we leave?"

"What do you mean?"

"You said my family is leading the search tomorrow. But I . . . I can't remember what time we're leaving."

"Your family?" Wiri looked puzzled. "Well, the men and older boys will leave at dawn, of course. They'll want to go as far as they can before it gets too hot."

"Men and boys?" said Keisha. "Aren't the girls going with them, too?"

"Of course not." Wiri made a face as if she'd never heard such a shocking idea in her whole life.

Chapter

Five

A
SECRET
PLAN

Wiri gestured for Keisha to follow her. She silently handed her two earthenware jugs and gave a smaller one to Sofi and one to Dona, her own little sister. Then she took two jugs and a large basket and walked out into the forest.

Keisha trudged along behind the others, trying to figure out what was so terrible about wanting to help find a new site for the village. She wished she knew exactly what part of Africa she was in and what year it was.

The farther they walked, the darker it got. When she looked up, Keisha couldn't see the sky at all, only tall, dark tree trunks and leaves in every shade of green. The only strong light was high overhead. Filtered through the endless trees, the light was deep green. Judging distances was impossible, and the air was so hot and moist that it was hard to breathe.

Keisha felt a little dizzy and sat down on the path. She jumped in surprise when she saw a pair of small brown feet just a few inches from her own. They were Sofi's.

"Come on, Kee-Kee. We're not far from the water now." Sofi tugged at her hand, and Keisha followed her to where Wiri and Dona stood waiting.

"I thought maybe you'd wandered off again," said Wiri, smiling. "I hope our new home will be this close to the river. These jugs are so heavy when they're filled." Wiri didn't seem at all unhappy about her task, though. She had barely finished the sentence before she ran ahead and scrambled up a tree. "Here, catch, Keisha!"

Several mangoes landed at Keisha's feet, spattering her legs, and her companions burst out laughing. Keisha loved the sweet, juicy, bright orange pulp of the fruit, and she gladly joined the little girls in eating it. Wiri, with perfect aim, tossed down a dozen more, and they placed them in Wiri's basket.

A Secret Plan

Soon the girls were
scooting down the riverbank
and filling their jugs. Wiri
gave the little girls
permission to swim for a few
minutes, and she and Keisha sat
down on the bank and dangled their
feet in the water.

"Wiri, I'm sorry I upset you earlier," said Keisha. "Tell
me, what's wrong with wanting to go exploring?"

"As girls, we have other things to do," Wiri replied
simply. "Why would you want to do something different?"

"I—I don't know," Keisha said. She wasn't sure how
to explain her feelings.

Wiri thought for a moment before she spoke.
"Well, you are Mukumu Mbele's only daughter, born of
his second wife. If you really want to go along, why
don't you ask your *babu* if he'll let you. Stranger things
have happened."

"Maybe I will," replied Keisha. "Or maybe I'll ask my *mama*."

"Well, it's obvious that your mother's spirit keeps
special watch over you, Keisha. But my mother says she
was one of the most respected women in the village, so I'm
not so sure her spirit would give you permission to do
something like that."

My mother must be dead, and the whole idea of my going shocks Wiri so much, thought Keisha.

Wiri laughed good-naturedly. "Come on. We'd better get back soon or something worse than a cold supper will be waiting for us." She shooed the little ones out of the water, and they all picked up their water jugs and fruit and headed back into the forest. As soon as they were on the path, Keisha took Sofi's hand. It helped Keisha keep her footing as they walked along.

Suddenly a bright light hit Keisha's eyes, and she had to squint hard. They had reached the clearing. The walk back seemed much shorter than the trip to the river had been. Keisha inhaled deeply as she entered the village. The air was filled with the smell of cooking. The only aromas she could identify for sure were fish and onions.

"Mmm," said Wiri, sniffing the air. "Nyam, *mbogoa*, and *ngonda*. And *vyura*, too. What a feast! The men did well on their fishing expedition."

Keisha frowned. She liked yams and vegetables and fish, but that didn't mean she'd like the way they were cooked. And she really wasn't sure she was adventurous enough to try eating *vyura*—that word meant "frogs!"

A Secret Plan

Several women were squatting around three open
dried-mud fire pits. Big pots were suspended over each
and the heat from the fires warmed Keisha's cheeks as she
stepped closer. She wiped a trickle of sweat from her
forehead and looked at Wiri to see what she should do.

One woman called out, "Come, respected fathers, and
eat." She served the men in turn: first the elders, then the
other grown men, then the boys. They all went to sit
together in front of the old men's huts. The server called
the old women next.

Finally the woman nodded to Wiri. Wiri went up and
took two bowls of stew and a helping of meat on a large,
stiff leaf. Then she sat on the ground a few paces from the
men's group.

A cocoa-colored man with a deep voice nodded at
Keisha and went on talking and eating. It was easy to tell
that he was Mukumu Mbele. It wasn't just that he wore
a beautiful leopard skin draped across his shoulders. There
was something about the way he carried himself—he held
his head extra high and proud, and everyone made room for
him—that told Keisha he must be the village leader.

Keisha picked up spoons and bowls and joined the end
of the line, wondering why all the girls her age took at least
two bowls. The other girls went to sit with Wiri, so Keisha
joined them. Within seconds, at least one younger child

appeared beside each girl, sat down, took her food from her nurse-sibling, and began to eat.

Now Keisha understood why the girls had taken more than one portion of food. She handed Sofi a bowl and all the frog meat, then looked at her own dish. It didn't look or smell quite like any stew her real mother had ever made. She hesitated for a moment, then tasted a small spoonful.

"This is delicious!" she exclaimed. Besides the herbs and vegetables and little bits of cooked fish, the stew contained peanuts. Keisha gladly accepted a second helping. She couldn't believe how hungry she was and how good the stew tasted. She thought she'd even try frog meat the next day if there was any left!

The women were eating in their own group. Keisha wondered why people didn't eat with their families, but she knew she couldn't ask about things like that.

With everyone chatting and laughing, Keisha couldn't catch much besides the girls' conversation. She did hear the men say something about heading north at dawn, and part of a discussion about how many spears to carry, but not much else.

When the meal was over, Mama Loma announced that after the girls cleaned up, they were free to play with the little ones. The boys would help finish the preparations for the next day's journey. Keisha worked silently, taking her cues from Wiri and doing her best to be helpful. Even the three-year-olds helped, and the meal was quickly cleared away.

"You go ahead and play," Keisha said to Sofi. "I'll join you soon." She had been thinking hard during cleanup. Someone had to find a new site for the village, and she knew who it was going to be: the only daughter of Mukumu Mbele! "Sofi," she called, "come to my hut—I need you to help me with something." Sofi's eyes lit up.

Keisha hardly had time to pick up the crown and collar as Sofi nearly dragged her to one of the huts.

Keisha looked at the low stacks of woven mats and thin blankets and the few pieces of clothing neatly folded beside each stack. "Sofi, which of my dresses is your favorite?" she asked.

Sofi ran to one bed and pulled an orange and brown dress from the pile. "This one looks prettiest on you," she said. "Why?"

Uh-oh, thought Keisha. What now? She walked over and looked through the small pile to give herself time to think. She took the dress from Sofi and held it up to the light.

"Well," Keisha finally said, "I wanted to wear something really nice to see my father on his way tomorrow." Sofi seemed satisfied with that, so Keisha said, "All right, you go join the other children. I'll be with you in a few minutes." Sofi just stood there looking at her.

"Sofi, go now," said Keisha. Her voice was a little sharper than she'd intended. Sofi's lips puckered and her shoulders fell, but she turned obediently and left the hut.

Keisha looked around a little more and found a brown

drawstring bag hanging on the wall. I'd better join the others before someone comes looking for me, she thought. She quickly folded the dress, put it in the bag, and hurried out the door.

"Keisha! *Njoni!* Come here!" Sofi shouted when Keisha reached the gate. "We're playing leopards-and-colobuses. And this time, we're the leopards and you're one of the monkeys."

It was easy enough for Keisha to guess what she was supposed to do. "Help!" Keisha shouted. "The leopards are after me!" She ran through the gate, with a small band of shrieking youngsters close behind.

By the time the panting, giggling "spotted leopards" and "colobus monkeys" returned, the whole village was settling down for the night. The girls quickly washed up and went to sit around the fires and listen to the grandmothers' storytelling. Keisha wished she could listen to them all night long. But when Mukumu Mbele stretched and stood up, the old women began to bank the fires and the adults said good night to everyone.

"Come on, Keisha," said Wiri, taking Dona in her arms.

"I never did get a chance to talk to Mukumu Mbele," Keisha mumbled to herself as she lay down, but she was too worn out to think about it. She curled up on her woven mat and instantly fell asleep.

Chapter Six

FINDING A FRIEND

Keisha woke to the sound of birds twittering and roosters crowing. She was sure she heard Mukumu Mbele's voice as she got dressed. The light inside the hut was very dim, but Keisha had set everything where she could find it easily. She stooped beside the mat and looked out the open doorway.

"Keisha, may I go with you?" said a tiny voice.

Keisha nearly lost her balance. "Sofi!" she cried softly. "Get back to bed."

"You left me behind again yesterday, and . . ." Sofi's eyes looked just like Ashley's did when she was trying not to cry.

Keisha picked her up and gave her a hug. "No, you must stay here." Sofi sniffled loudly. Keisha thought fast. "Listen," she whispered. "I'm counting on you to be a big girl and keep this our secret. Can you do it?"

Sofi nodded, but she still looked tearful. Keisha stroked the little girl's soft, curly hair. "I'm sure the grandmothers will tell you stories while I'm gone. Maybe someday there will even be a story about how a little girl named Sofi helped the *mukumu*'s daughter do something very important."

Sofi managed a smile as Keisha tucked her into bed. "Now you go on back to sleep and don't worry about a thing." She gave Sofi a quick kiss, picked up the bag, and stepped into the doorway.

The last of the men were just going out the gate. Keisha made sure no one was in the cooking area, then hurried over and got a small jug of fresh water, a handful of dried fish, some fruit, and a large piece of flatbread. She stuffed them into the bag and walked quickly to the clearing outside the village. She looked around, then turned north and walked into the forest.

After only a few minutes, everything looked fuzzy and unreal, and Keisha became as dizzy as the day before. She stopped to take some deep breaths and practiced focusing her vision just a few feet ahead. That helped quite a bit. As she took a small sip of water, she thought she heard laughter. She picked up the bag and began walking again. Soon she heard the deep voice of Mukumu Mbele somewhere ahead. Boys were laughing and joking, and it sounded like someone was chopping wood: The men must be clearing the path as they went along. Keisha hadn't even noticed until then that there were freshly cut branches lying beside the trail. Now it was easy to follow the search party.

The light gradually increased a little as she traveled. It had that same strange green cast as the day before, but in a few places it now penetrated all the way down to the lowest shrubs. A huge butterfly slowly opened and closed its wings atop a flower that looked like a magnolia. Keisha wanted to go close to sniff it, but she didn't want to frighten the butterfly away. She stood watching for a few moments, enchanted, then hurried on so she wouldn't fall too far behind.

After awhile, Keisha stopped again, listening hard and

staring into the gloom. She felt as if someone were hiding there, watching her. Had the *mukumu* heard her stumbling along behind the search party and told someone to send her back to the village? Or was some animal waiting to ambush her?

She peered into the shadows and gathered up her courage. Slowly, carefully, she stepped closer. It was a person—a woman in tattered clothing, sitting slumped against a tree. Even in the gloom of the forest, her hair shone nearly white.

Finding a Friend

"Bibi? Grandmother?"

The old woman stared at Keisha for a moment, then smiled weakly. "*Jambo, mwanango. Njoni*," she said. "Hello, my child. Come here."

Keisha squatted beside the woman. "Why are you all alone in the forest?" she asked.

"How can an old widow make such a young girl understand? I am a very poor woman, without a family. I have no children to love me, and my husband was too poor to afford other wives. There is no one to inherit me, to take care of me now that I am old and sick and my husband is dead. There's no one to remember me as a respected ancestor after I die. I am waiting for the spirits to take me away."

Keisha had no idea what to say. She felt terrible. She uncorked her small jug of water and held it to the woman's lips. The woman weakly tipped the jug and sipped at the water, but she refused the banana that Keisha offered. She sighed gratefully and patted Keisha's hand.

"Tell me, my child, why are you here? Surely you aren't alone."

"It's time to find a new site for our village," Keisha replied. Then she added proudly, "I want to be the one who finds it."

The old woman frowned. "And what about your duties at home? Who's doing your work for you?"

Keisha didn't answer.

"What is your name?"

"Keisha."

"Mine is Isubu."

Keisha said the name softly: "Ee-soo-boo. I like the sound of it."

"Thank you for the water, Keisha. You'd best go home now. You must have little ones to take care of, and they need you."

"Oh, the other girls can do that, Isubu. I . . . well, I want to do something *important*," Keisha said. "I don't know why no one seems to understand that."

"What makes you think your work is not important?" the old woman asked. "Even I had something to give my village: I told the stories of the ancient times to the children and rocked the babies so their mothers were free to do their work. Now my time is nearly over, but you still have a great many things to do for your people. One of the most important is to learn all you can and do your part well." The old woman began to cough.

Keisha sat mulling over what Isubu had said. She

picked up a leaf and turned it over and over on her palm, then peeked over at Isubu and watched her for awhile. The woman was so weak and old, she looked as if she could barely hold her head up.

"Isubu, please let me take you to my village."

The old woman stared at Keisha. "Have you given up your search, then?" she asked.

"I thought about what you said," Keisha replied. "My family does need me, and in the village we can take good care of you."

"You're a good child, and I thank you. But I'll stay here and wait for the spirits."

Keisha had never seen such sadness in anyone's face before. Isubu probably would die if she left her alone. "Please come, Isubu," she pleaded. "I want to hear your stories of the ancient times. You can . . . you can be *our* grandmother. . . .
Please, *Bibi*."
She took the
woman's
hands and
carefully
pulled her to her
feet. "We need you."

Chapter

Seven

THE
JOURNEY
HOME

Keisha and Isubu had to stop often so the old
woman could catch her breath. Sometimes Keisha
practically had to carry her. The sun was directly
overhead, and it was too hot to go on without a rest.
Keisha helped Isubu get as comfortable as she could
under the shade of a young, low-growing mango tree.
Then she put her gymnastics and cheerleading training to
good use, shinnying up the tree and snagging a few fruits.
The old woman wanted only a taste of a mango.

"Tell me, Keisha," said Isubu, "what is your place among your people?"

Keisha was about to tell Isubu about her real family when she remembered that the old woman wouldn't know what she was talking about. She simply answered, "I am the chief's only daughter."

"You're part of an important family. And your mother?"

"She died when I was born."

"Your father must love you very much."

"I—I suppose he loves all his children. And he's always there when we need him."

"You are so lucky to have such a father. Why do you sound so doubtful, my child?"

Keisha just had to explain, to make someone understand how she felt. "Well, because all I get to do is take care of the little ones and help with chores," she replied. "Who cares if I can sweep or wash dishes or play tag with the babies? My father is so busy and so important, sometimes I think he doesn't even notice me."

"Keisha, don't be foolish," Isubu said. "He may seem too busy for you sometimes, but I think you know deep down that he loves you with all his heart."

Keisha couldn't help thinking of her real father. Her mother had told her that he checked her room and blew her a kiss every night on his way to bed, no matter how late it was. And his smile was so warm when he greeted her every day after work, even when he looked tired.

Keisha helped the old woman up and slowly led her out of the sweltering, shadowy forest.

When they were a few feet from the village gate, Wiri came running up. "Keisha!" she exclaimed. "Where were you this time? Sofi is in tears and won't talk to anyone, and Mama Loma is going crazy with worry about you." Then she looked at Isubu and fell silent.

The old woman tried to stand straight and tall, leaning heavily on Keisha's arm. "My name is . . .," she began, but a fit of coughing doubled her over.

"This is Isubu, my new grandmother," said Keisha. "I found her alone in the forest."

Wiri gestured respectfully to Isubu. "Welcome, Bibi Isubu. Let me tell the elders that you're here." She gave Keisha a quick questioning look, then dashed away. Just moments later, several women led Isubu into the coolest of the women's huts while Mama Loma took Keisha aside.

"Keisha! You've neglected your duties again!" She looked sternly at Keisha, her hands on her hips. "I don't know where you found this unfortunate Isubu, but as soon as you and the women get her settled, go see to poor Sofi. She's been crying for you all day." Mama Loma glanced inside the hut, and when she spoke again her voice was a little softer. "At least you seem to have learned *one* lesson. We'll talk about your duties later."

"Yes, Mama Loma," Keisha replied. She went inside and helped make Isubu as comfortable as she could. The old woman immediately drifted into an exhausted sleep.

Keisha checked on Isubu several times, but the old woman didn't awaken until long after supper had been cleared away. Keisha's face lit up when she saw that Isubu's eyes were finally open, and she said softly, "I'll be right back." She hurried out to find Mama Loma.

"Bibi Isubu is awake," Keisha announced. "I have to give her some food."

Mama Loma clucked her tongue and started to say something. Then she seemed to change her mind, and she dished out a bowl of broth and handed it to Keisha.

"But shouldn't she have some fish? It's so full of"— Keisha almost said "vitamins and protein" but caught herself in time—"good things to make you strong."

Mama Loma smoothed Keisha's hair and said gently, "See if she can take a drink first."

When Keisha reentered the hut and sat down beside

Isubu, the old woman was shaking so badly that Keisha
had to lift her head and help her drink the broth.

Isubu lay back on the mat and felt around inside her
dress, eventually pulling out a small leather pouch.
"Keisha, this is for you. I was going to present it to you
when your father returns, but the voices of my ancestors
tell me to give it to you now."

"I don't need a gift, Isubu. I'm just glad you're
feeling better."

A little smile crossed Isubu's face. "You may not

need this gift," she said, "but I want you to have it."

Keisha opened the drawstring, reached inside the little pouch, and took out a beautifully carved wooden comb and a mirror with a decorated wooden handle. "Oh, Isubu! I've never had such a wonderful gift!" Keisha cried.

"When you look in the mirror," said Isubu, "I hope you will see how kindhearted you are. And I hope you will always remember your adopted ancestor."

"Of course I will, Bibi Isubu," said Keisha. "I know you'll have a lot of stories to tell me and the other children around the fire when you feel better."

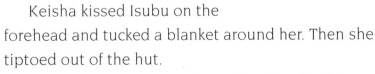

Isubu took the comb and set it into Keisha's hair. "I'm very tired, Keisha. I am going to rest now."

Keisha kissed Isubu on the forehead and tucked a blanket around her. Then she tiptoed out of the hut.

The next morning, Keisha tied Isubu's leather pouch to her waist and went to fix the old woman some peeled mango and boiled yam. She mashed the yam until it was very soft, so Isubu wouldn't have to chew it.

"Good morning, Grandmother Isubu," she said cheerily, setting the plate beside the bed. When the old woman didn't stir, Keisha tapped her shoulder gently and greeted her a little more loudly. Isubu still didn't move.

Keisha ran out of the hut. "Mama Loma!" she cried. "I'm afraid, Mama Loma. Bibi Isubu . . ."

They hurried to the hut together, and Mama Loma squatted beside the mat and looked closely at Isubu. Then she turned to Keisha.

"My child, Bibi Isubu has gone to join the ancestors."

"But I thought she was better. I thought that bringing her here and taking care of her . . . I wanted to hear her stories." Keisha burst into tears.

"Don't be sad, Keisha. She is happy now, and she will watch over you all your life," said Mama Loma. She held Keisha tightly and let her cry. Finally she led her out and sat her down beside Wiri, nodded toward the hut where Isubu lay, then walked quietly away.

Wiri took Keisha's hand. "Keisha, the men have returned," she said softly.

Keisha wiped her eyes. "Did they find good land?"

"Yes, they did. We'll begin packing up the day after Bibi Isubu's ceremony."

"Where's Mukumu Mbele—my father? I have to go apologize for being disobedient."

"Mama Loma already explained everything to him. Everyone heard him say he was proud that you brought Bibi Isubu home and gave her a family to honor her memory. At the burial ceremony tomorrow, he's going to declare her a respected ancestor of our community."

Keisha couldn't get the lump out of her throat enough to say anything.

"Everyone says Bibi Isubu was sent to protect you and bring you good fortune. She'll help the spirit of your mother and of all your other ancestors watch over you." Wiri was silent for a moment, then squeezed Keisha's hand and stood up. "Why don't you rest for awhile until you feel better. I'll go check on the little ones and help start dinner, and I'll come see how you are later."

Keisha stood, too, and gave Wiri a big hug. "Thank you, Wiri. You've made me feel a little better already. And you've been awfully kind to me—about everything."

Wiri patted Keisha on the shoulder and ran off across the yard. Keisha let herself take a last, long look around the village. Then she walked slowly to the hut, removed the mirror from the little pouch, and set it on Sofi's bed. She gazed down at her reflection. It was time to go home.

Chapter Eight

A WAY
TO REMEMBER

Ellie's attic seemed very quiet as Keisha put on her own clothes and replaced the outfit in the trunk. Her jeans felt tight and uncomfortable after the loose, flowing robe. She dusted her feet, wishing she didn't have to put her shoes back on.

Keisha lowered the lid of the trunk and walked to the mirror. Lying right in front of it was the lovely comb that Isubu had given her. She ran down the steps, locked the door, and sped on down to the ground floor—and nearly knocked Ellie down at the foot of the stairs.

"Oh, Ellie, I'm sorry! Are you all right?" she asked.

"Fine, dear." Ellie laughed as she knelt to pick up a large book she had dropped and led Keisha into the sitting room. "Did you find anything interesting?"

"Did I! I was in a village in the rain forest. But wait until I show you what I found when I got back." Keisha handed Ellie the comb.

Ellie examined it. "Oh, this is a very fine old hair pick. You should treasure it, dear." She folded Keisha's fingers around the smooth, dark wood.

Keisha's eyes shone as she gave Ellie a big hug.

Ellie smiled, then leafed through the big book. She laid it flat and placed a finger in the middle of the page. It showed a map of Africa, and she was pointing to the second-largest river system on the whole continent.

The grandfather clock chimed in the hallway, and Keisha jumped up. It was time to go home. "Oh, no! I'd better hurry or I'm going to be late for dinner," she said. "Bye, Ellie."

Keisha raced home. "Hi, sorry I'm late," she said.

"That's all right, honey," said Mrs. Vance. "Are you feeling better?"

Keisha looked at her mother in astonishment. "How did you know I was upset?"

"Don't forget I'm your mom. I know you better than anyone else does."

"This is kind of hard to say, Mama." Keisha hesitated, then plunged in. "You and Dad do such important work, you know, and all I really do is go to school and baby-sit Ashley and Ronnie. And, well, I was worried that you and Daddy didn't really . . ." Keisha scuffed her toes on the linoleum.

Mrs. Vance hugged Keisha very close. "Oh, baby, you mustn't ever wonder how we feel about you. You don't have to do anything but be our Keisha-girl." She rubbed her cheek against Keisha's hair. "Besides," she went on, "your father and I couldn't make it through a single day without you. You're the hero of the household."

"I am?"

"Certainly. But I guess maybe we don't give you a lot of thanks—"

"Mommy! I'm hungry!" Ronnie announced, barreling into the kitchen.

Mrs. Vance gave Keisha a helpless look. "Keisha, how

about if we talk some more later, all right?"

"Sure, Mom. I'll get Dad and Ashley." Keisha went to the family room. "Dinner's ready," she said, then walked over to her father and threw her arms around his neck. "That was an exciting talk you gave today, Daddy. Everyone was really caught up in your stories. I was so proud of you."

"I do tell a pretty good story, don't I?" Mr. Vance said with a smile. "But you seemed upset after school, kitten. Did I do something wrong?"

"Go on and wash up, Ash," said Keisha. When Ashley didn't move, Mr. Vance gave her a stern look. She left the room, and Keisha sat down on the arm of her father's chair. "I felt like taking care of Ronnie and Ashley wasn't very exciting or important, and I guess I was feeling sort of left out. But I've thought about it a lot, and everything is okay now. I found out all of us have our special jobs that make this family work."

"I'm glad," said Mr. Vance, "because you know you're my favorite older daughter." They laughed as he put his arm around Keisha and went into the kitchen.

During dessert, Keisha made an announcement. "Tonight I'm putting Ashley and Ronnie to bed. I have a special bedtime story to tell them."

"Can we hear it now?" Ashley asked eagerly.

"Nope." Keisha smiled and tugged at the beads in her sister's braids. "We have to wait until you've had your bath and you're all tucked in. This is a super-special bedtime story that comes all the way from Africa!"

Diary

Dear Diary:

Whew! A lot has happened since the last time I wrote. First, my dad came to school and gave a talk about being a paramedic. The class thought it was <u>soooo</u> cool.

The next day I got to volunteer at the hospital where my mom and dad work. I spent the whole morning helping old folks. When I first walked in, I didn't think I was going to have any fun, but I did. There was one man named Mr. Parsons who was a hoot and a half. He kept teasing the ladies about taking them dancing and to the movies. Some of them actually blushed! He asked me to write postcards to his grandchildren because he can't hold a pen so steady anymore, and I could tell from what he said that he really loved them and missed them. Later I read the newspaper out loud to everyone, and Mr. Parsons helped me with the hard words.

But the best thing was my visit to Ellie's attic. I told Ali and Heather and Megan all about it, of course, and we still can't believe I wound up in Africa! It was better and more wonderful than anything I could have imagined, and I met people I will never ever forget, especially Isubu.

I'm glad I met Isubu before I volunteered in the hospital. She and all the people in the village helped me understand how important it is to do your part and to take time out to help others.

I went to the library and took out a few books about Africa. Some of the dresses looked a lot like the one I wore. I showed Mama the comb (but I didn't tell her how I really got it) and she said it was exquisite. Then she reminded me to write Ellie a thank-you note, so I did. After all, without her I wouldn't have it.

I was amazed to see how different the parts of Africa are. I mean, probably everybody knows that the biggest desert in the world is there. But I never knew there are mountains and plains and rain forests, too. I guess I never really thought about it very much until now. I only got to see a very small part of Africa in my adventure, and I just <u>have</u> to see more sometime. Maybe one of these days our whole family can go there for a long trip.

Well, I hear Mama telling me to turn out my light and go to sleep. So . . .

Bye, Diary!

Keisha

Learn
More
About It

CENTRAL AFRICA TODAY

K eisha Leads the Way is set in ancient central Africa, the land of the great Congo River basin. Long ago, the people who lived in the steamy rain forests and on the hot, grassy plains were both hunters and farmers. They moved their villages every few years to find more fertile croplands and better hunting grounds, using the many rivers as "highways." As they encountered other clans and tribes in their travels, new cultures, customs, and languages were formed.

Time has brought many changes, and that way of life no longer exists. A little over 100 years ago, the powerful countries of Europe conquered and divided most of Africa into colonies. The Congo River basin fell under the control of Belgium and France. In the mid-1900s, however, native Africans began to demand their own free governments. As a result, in the 1960s, several newly independent countries emerged: the Central African Republic, the Congo, Equatorial Guinea, and Gabon. By the end of the decade, the Congo had been renamed

Zaire, and today the Congo River basin is often called the Zaire River basin.

One of the richest countries in the region is Gabon (guh-BONE). Most of the land is covered by dense rain forest. Farmers there raise cocoa and coffee beans to sell throughout the world. Oil is a valuable natural resource, so the country's small population makes a great deal more money than most Africans do. The capital of Libreville (LEE-bruh-vil), with its busy traffic and modern skyscrapers, looks a lot like many American cities. French is the official language.

Zaire (zah-YEAR) is like Gabon in some ways: Its main language is French, part of the land is tropical rain forest, and coffee and cocoa are raised for export. But in other ways the two countries are very different. There are no large oil deposits to bring wealth to the millions of people living in Zaire; in fact, it is one of the poorest nations in the world. Zaire's capital, Kinshasa (kin-SHAW-suh), is larger than Seattle or Boston, but it is not very modern. Most of its 4 million inhabitants are very poor and live in shacks.

All children in both Zaire and Gabon go to grade school. They learn reading and writing, and arithmetic. Schools in the cities are a lot like the ones in the United States, with morning and afternoon classes, and recesses, when students get a chance to play sports and games. In the farming villages, where most of the people in both countries still live, schools are usually one-room houses, so students are not separated into grades. Many village schools run only half a day, so there is no recess.

But going to school for just half the day doesn't mean that students can play when they get home. Instead, they have to help their parents do the farmwork and housework. When the chores are done, they usually eat dinner and go to bed soon afterward. There is no electricity, so they have no electric lights, televisions, stereos or CD players, or computers.

After they finish the fourth or fifth grade, most students have to quit school and work full-time to help their families survive. Only about one sixth of the children in Zaire and one third of those in Gabon get to go on to high school and study science or foreign languages such as English. The few who attend college—about two or three out of every 100—often travel to Europe or the United States to attend a university.

In the African village in this story, the roles that people are expected to play are very traditional ones—women stay home to take care of family, and men go out to farm, hunt, and explore. But this is not true in every African society, any more than it is true in ours.

BANTU GLOSSARY

B antu is the name of a group of languages that have been spoken in various parts of Africa for thousands of years. The words in Keisha's story are real Bantu words, but they come from a lot of different Bantu languages rather than from just one.

baba - father
bibi - grandmother
ewe - you there
jambo - hello
mama - mother
mukumu - chief
mbogoa - vegetable(s)
mwanango - my child
ngonda - dried fish
njoni - come here

nkanga (*plural of kanga*) - guinea fowl, a native African bird related to pheasants
nyam - yam(s), an edible root similar to sweet potatos
Uwa na nchovu - Good morning
vyura (*plural of kyura*) - frogs

Central Africa Today

Geographical

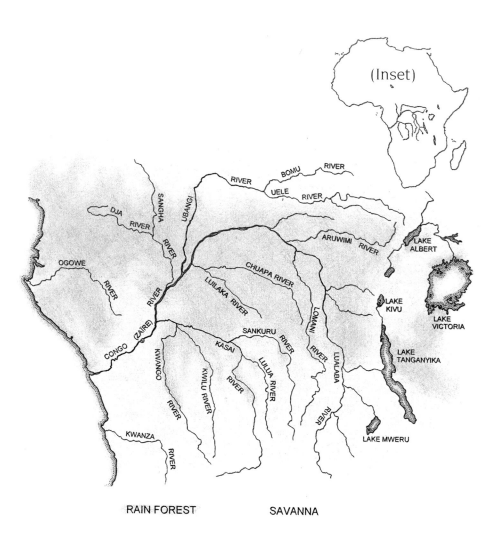

(Inset)

RAIN FOREST   SAVANNA

Countries

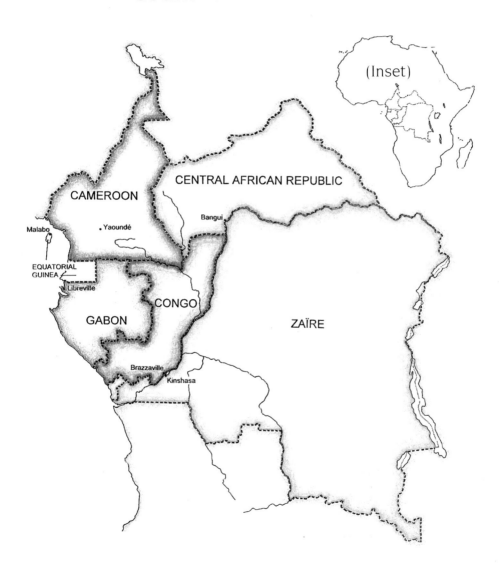